Alex
the Super
Soccer Striker

Peter Millett
Illustrated by Wayne Bryant

Contents

Chapter 1
The Newest Class Member

Alexandra Johnson was feeling very shy. Her family had moved into a new neighborhood, and it was her first day at a new school.

Alexandra stood next to the teacher, Mr. Simpson, and looked down at her shoes. She didn't want to look up at the faces of the other children staring at her.

"Good morning, class," said Mr. Simpson, in a loud, friendly voice. "I would like you to welcome the newest member of our class, Alexandra Johnson."

Alexandra was sure her cheeks were turning red. She slowly lifted her head and looked toward the back of the class.

"So, Alexandra, tell us where you're from," said Mr. Simpson, smiling at her.

Alexandra looked up at him, feeling slightly breathless. "Um, from a different city . . . really far away from here," she murmured.

"Interesting," Mr. Simpson said. "Is there anything else you would like to tell us about yourself today?"

Alexandra slowly shook her head.
"Not really," she replied.

"No problem," said Mr. Simpson. "Why don't you sit at that table, and we'll get you settled into our routines in no time at all." He pointed to a table in the middle of the classroom.

Alexandra took a seat next to a tall boy with dark hair.

"Zach," said Mr. Simpson, "you'll make Alexandra feel right at home this morning, won't you?"

"Yep," Zach said, nodding.

Alexandra smiled politely at Mr. Simpson and took out a pen from her pencil case.

Mr. Simpson began writing energetically on the whiteboard. He wrote: *soccer, table tennis, hockey, baseball.*

"All right, everyone," said Mr. Simpson. "This is a final reminder. If you are interested in playing any of these sports, you will need to write your name on the sign-up sheet on the bulletin board outside this classroom. The sheet will be up until three o'clock this afternoon. Be quick or you will miss out."

At the end of class, Mr. Simpson walked over to Alexandra and smiled at her.

"Are you interested in playing sports at our school?" he asked.

Alexandra nodded shyly but didn't say anything.

Zach, who was wearing a soccer shirt, swung around in his chair. "Let me guess," he said to Alexandra. "You play either hockey or table tennis?"

Alexandra coughed into her hand. "Maybe," she whispered.

Chapter 2
The Top Eleven

The next morning, there was a small crowd gathered around the bulletin board. Everybody was interested to see who had put their names on the list to try out for the different sports teams.

The most popular sport was soccer. There were more names on the soccer list than the eleven positions available for the team.

The soccer coach, Ms. Jackson, walked past the group and smiled. "Why do I have a feeling this year is going to be our best year ever?" she asked. "I have never seen so much interest in soccer. I wonder who is going to be good enough to make the final team."

"Ooh, I will," said Michael.

"No, I will," said Cory.

Zach was the best soccer player in the school. He had won the Player of the Year award last year. He moved toward the front of the crowd and tapped the list. He had a curious expression on his face.

"Hey, who are these two guys?" Zach pointed at the two names scribbled at the bottom of the list. "Alex and Noah? I've never heard of them before. Do you think they are any good?" he asked, looking at the other boys.

"Let's hope so. They might even be as good as you," Ms. Jackson laughed. "Maybe our soccer team will have a new captain this year?"

"I don't think so, Ms. Jackson," said Zach, confidently. "I scored ten goals last season, and I plan on scoring ten more this season. That's going to be difficult to beat if you want to be the number-one striker on our team."

"We'll see," said Ms. Jackson. "Maybe we are in for some surprises this year, Zach."

Just then, the bell rang to signal the start of the school day.

"Oops!" Ms. Jackson moved quickly aside to avoid a girl with red hair darting past her.

"Hey, slow down," she said. "This isn't a racing track. You could fall over and give yourself a nasty injury."

"Sorry," Alexandra said, as she weaved past the children standing around the bulletin board and walked into the classroom. "I can't believe I'm late on just my second day here," she said under her breath.

Chapter 3
Soccer Tryouts

After school, a group of boys gathered on the field to wait for the soccer tryouts. They were wearing their soccer cleats. Everyone was wondering who would make the team and be in the top eleven. Ms. Jackson read aloud their names from the list on her clipboard.

"Liam, Cory . . ."

"Here," the two boys replied.

"Zach, Michael . . ."

"Here!" Zach and Michael shouted.

"Noah, Alex . . ."

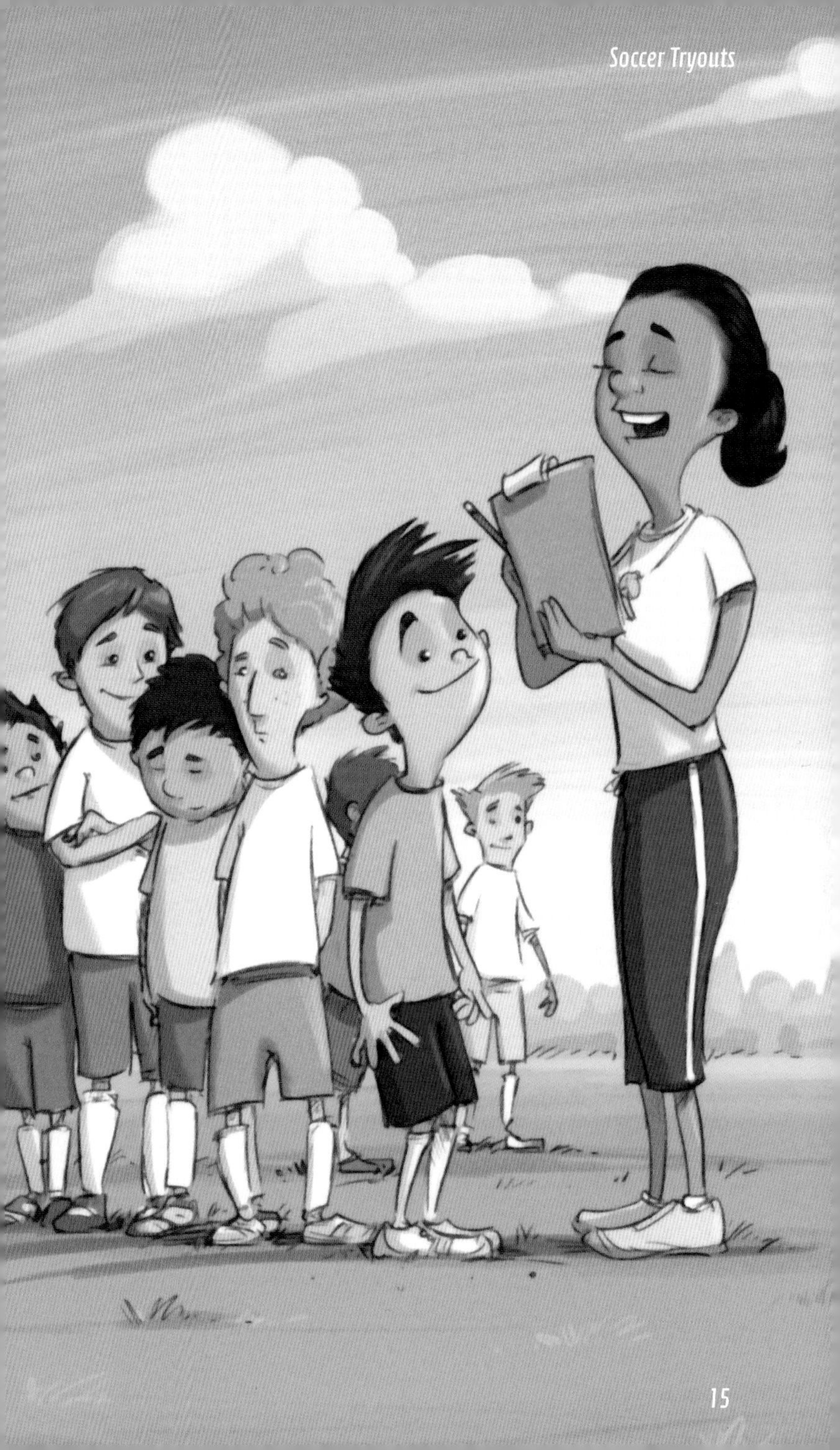

No one replied. A few moments later, two players came sprinting across the field from near the library.

Zach was puzzled to see the new girl in his class running toward them, wearing soccer cleats and shin guards.

"Noah, Alex . . ." the coach repeated.

"Here," Noah called.

"Here," Alexandra said breathlessly.

"What? You're Alex?" Zach exclaimed in surprise.

Alexandra smiled. "Yep. My friends call me Alex. This is my brother, Noah."

Noah waved at Zach.

Zach looked at Alexandra. "Are you sure you've picked the right sport?" he asked. "In case you didn't notice, there aren't any other girls here."

Alexandra looked around. "Wow, you're right," she replied with a grin. "You're really observant. No, there don't seem to be any other girls around here. Where are they?"

Zach looked confused. "Um . . . did you play for the soccer team at your old school?"

Alexandra shook her head. "No," she said.

"So today is the first time you've ever tried out for a school soccer team?" asked Zach.

"Yes," Alexandra said, with a broad smile.

"Uh-huh," said Zach thoughtfully.

"Okay, students, let's stop the chatter," Ms. Jackson said briskly. "It's time for you to show me what you can do on the field. We'll begin with a scrimmage. I'll split you into two teams and see how you play."

Chapter 4

The Moment of Truth

PHEEEEWP! The coach blew her whistle and the game began.

Alexandra was playing as a striker up front, near the goal net. She was on the same team as Zach.

"Hey, aren't you a little short to be playing as a striker?" Zach quipped.

"No," Alexandra responded. "I'm almost as tall as Leonardo Rezzi. You have heard of him, haven't you? He's a pretty good striker, don't you think?"

Zach nodded. "All right, let's see what you can do then."

A moment later, a ball came flying through the midfield toward Alexandra. Zach quickly intercepted the pass and started dribbling it wide by himself.

"Hey," Alexandra said, frowning. "That was my ball." She put her head down and chased him. "I'm free behind you," she cried, catching up to Zach.

However, Zach ignored Alexandra's call. Instead, he kept running at a fast speed along the sideline. But he ran too far ahead and found himself cornered by three defenders. He spun around and took a massive longshot at the goal from right next to the sideline. The shot missed, and the ball flew high and wide over the goalkeeper and the net.

Noah ran over to his sister. Alexandra was gritting her teeth.

"That was a wasted shot," she moaned. "Why didn't Zach pass the ball to me? He was never going to score a goal from that difficult position."

"Hey, Alex," Noah replied. "I think you're going to have to make a bit of noise on the field if you want to get the ball away from that boy today."

"You could be right," Alexandra sighed.

Chapter 5
Super Striker

By the second half of the game, Alexandra was becoming more confident. She knew she was as fast as the rest of the players—and sometimes, even faster.

Looking over her shoulder, she saw that one of the midfielders on her team was about to be caught from behind.

"HEY, LOOK OUT!" she bellowed.

Noah looked very surprised—he'd never heard his sister shout that loudly before.

The midfielder immediately passed the ball to another player.

"MINE, MINE!" Alexandra shouted at the boy with the ball, waving her hands. He fired a low, fast pass to Alexandra's left foot. She looked over to her right and saw Zach being closely pursued by another player.

"Hey, pass it to me," Zach pleaded.

Alexandra turned away from Zach and took a deep breath.

Using her heel, she kicked the ball a few yards to her left. Then she ran around two defenders to collect the ball and sprinted straight toward the goal box. She skilfully turned to her right and dodged a block.

Finally, she kicked the ball low and hard through the goalkeeper's legs and into the back of the net.

Zach looked stunned.

Ms. Jackson cheered noisily from the sidelines. "A brilliant goal! Remember I told you to slow down the other day? Well, you can ignore that on the field," she laughed. "I want you to run faster."

Noah ran over and congratulated his sister. "Nice, very nice," he said proudly, as he patted her on the back.

Zach jogged over to Alexandra. "I thought you said you'd never played for a school soccer team before?"

"I haven't," Alexandra replied with a smile. "That's because I normally play club soccer. I was far too busy on the weekends to play for my school team, too. But since I'm living in a new neighborhood, I thought I might as well try out for the team here at the school."

Zach gave Alexandra a high five.

"You dribble and shoot just like Leonardo Rezzi," he said. "Maybe even better!"

Alexandra could barely contain her grin.

Chapter 6

Announcing the Big News

At the end of the week, Ms. Jackson made her decision about which students made the soccer team.

There were two new members added to the team: Noah and Alex.

Alexandra hugged her brother when she saw the team list on the bulletin board.

"Well done, little sis," Noah grinned. "We'll have to give you the nickname 'lightning legs' now, won't we?"

Zach stopped in front of the bulletin board.

"Nice work, Alexandra," he said quietly, as he went into the classroom.

Alexandra followed closely behind Zach and sat down in her usual seat.

Mr. Simpson stood in front of the whiteboard.

"Well, class, it's news time," he said. "What's happening in your lives? Who's got something interesting to share before we start the day?"

Alexandra put her hand up immediately. Everyone looked at her in surprise.

"I do! I made the soccer team," she said excitedly.

Mr. Simpson looked pleased.

"Really? That's fantastic—especially since you've only been at our school for a few days. Well done! And thanks for sharing your news with the class, Alexandra."

Mr. Simpson turned to Zach. "So, Zach, you have some competition now. How do you feel about that?"

Zach looked over at Alexandra. "Good . . . I'm worried about one thing, though—I think Alexandra's going to score more goals than me this season!"

That weekend, the soccer team prepared to play their opening game of the season. Zach walked toward the center line with the soccer ball in his hand. He smiled at Alexandra and handed the ball to her.

"All yours," Zach said. "You can do the kick-off today." He extended his right arm to shake the newest team member's hand.

"Good luck, Alexandra," he said.

Alexandra shook Zach's hand warmly and beamed.

"Call me Alex," she said.